HELP WANTED

MUST LOVE BOOKS

written by
Janet Sumner Johnson

art by
Courtney Dawson

CAPSTONE EDITIONS
a capstone imprint

Help Wanted: Must Love Books is published by
Capstone Editions, a Capstone imprint
1710 Roe Crest Drive
North Mankato, Minnesota 56003
www.capstonepub.com

Library of Congress Cataloging-in-Publication Data
is available on the Library of Congress website.

ISBN 978-1-68446-075-5 (hardcover)
ISBN 978-1-68446-076-2 (eBook PDF)

Summary: Shailey loves bedtime, especially reading with her dad. But her dad starts
a new job, and it gets in the way of their bedtime routine. So Shailey takes action!
She fires her dad, posts a Help Wanted sign, and starts interviews immediately. She is
thrilled when her favorite characters from fairy tales line up to apply. But Sleeping Beauty
can't stay awake, the Gingerbread Man steals her book, and Snow White brings along her
whole team. Shailey is running out of options. Is bedtime ruined forever?

Designer: Brann Garvey

Printed and bound in China.
002491

To Girlie, who knows what she
wants and works for it.

—J.J.

Unlike most kids, Shailey loved bedtime.

She'd shimmy into her pj's,

brush her sparkling smile,

then raid the bookshelf for
the perfect bedtime stories.

Her dad would squish into the rocker with her, and they'd read until her eyelids refused to stay open.

This arrangement

worked perfectly . . .

. . . until her dad got a new job.

Finally, Shailey
reached her limit.

"You're fired!"
she announced.

She put up a job notice first thing the next morning . . .

. . . and began interviews
shortly before bedtime.

The fierce competition scared off the first three applicants.

The next applicant brought along her seven bodyguards,
which was fine—until Shailey offered them snacks.

Apply within. →

Interviews begin promptly at 6:30 p.m.

Shailey refused to interview any other applicants that night.

Before going to bed, she added a line to her job notice.

Help Wanted:

Bedtime Storyteller.

Must love books.
Apply within. →

Individual applicants only!

Interviews begin
promptly at 6:30 p.m.

The next night, the first applicant seemed delightful . . .

. . . until he ran away with the book.

Fee, fi, fo, fum! I hear the yawn of a tired one.

Shailey refused to come out from under the bed to interview applicant number two.

In the morning, Shailey changed her sign again.

At the next interview, Shailey's ears pricked right up. The applicant could spin tales that kept her on pins on needles. She was just about to offer the job, when the woman zonked out mid-sentence.

The second girl was very particular about where she would sit.

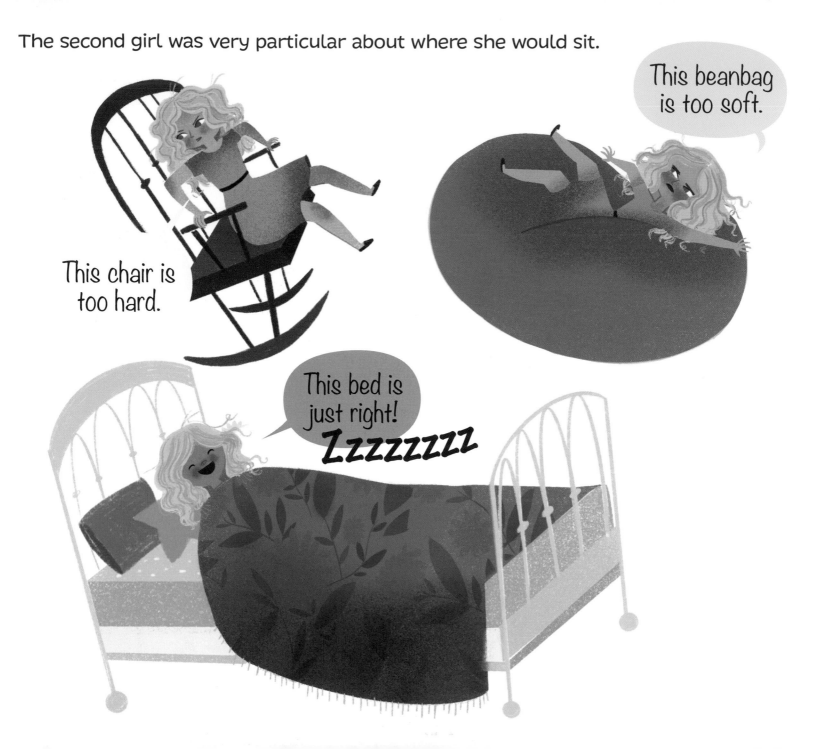

Help Wanted:
Bedtime Storyteller.
Must love books.
Apply within.
Individual applicants only!
Human applicants only.
Must be able to stay awake past 8 p.m.
Interviews begin promptly at 6:30 p.m.

Shailey had low expectations for the next round.

But the first applicant had a very impressive résumé.
Her voice was musical, she could stay up past midnight,
and she was obviously human.

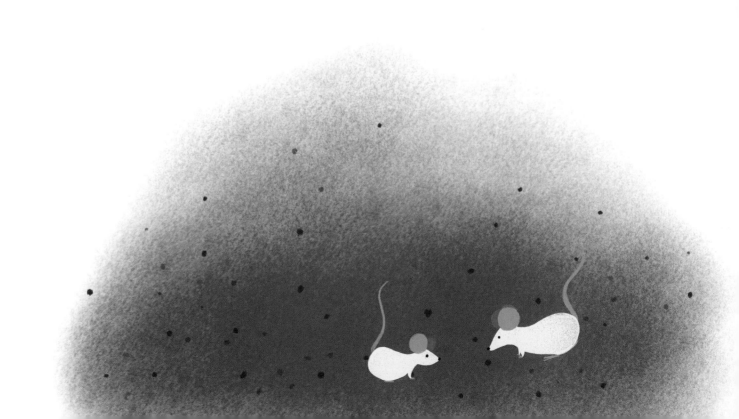

The two of them had a ball, until
Shailey noticed the sooty fingerprints
all over her favorite book.

The second applicant hooked
her right away. His storytelling
gave her goosebumps . . .

. . . as did the gunk
between his teeth.

Help Wanted:

Bedtime Storyteller.

Must love books.
Apply within. →

Individual applicants only!
Human applicants only.

Must be able
to stay awake
past 8 p.m.

Solid hygiene
skills required.

Interviews begin
promptly at 6:30 p.m.

Shailey despaired of ever finding

a replacement for her dad . . .

. . . until one final
job seeker showed up.

He looked kind of familiar, and his voice was just right. Best of all, he smelled like strawberries and chocolate chip cookies.

So Shailey offered him the job.

On ONE condition:

Pinocchio

Personal Statement
I have been reading for a long time. I mean, reading is something that is fun. I love reading bedtime stories. I have a lot . . . I mean *some* . . . I mean, *a little* . . . FINE! The truth is I can't read. I never went to school.

Highlights
- Knows how to have a whale of a time
- willing to do a trial period, no strings attached

Education
Do I really need to fill out this section?

Interests
learning to read, having a small nose, becoming a real boy

References
- Geppetto
- The Blue Fairy (maybe call her last . . . or not at all)

Robin Hood

◎ **Personal Statement**
It would truly be a feather in my cap to become your bedtime storyteller, but I'll get straight to the point. I am a wanted man, and my price is going up. Consider hiring me before I am—I mean, before my schedule—is all tied up.

◎ **Highlights**
- stories always hit the mark
- known for making others merry
- negotiable fee (based on economic status)

◎ **Interests**
lifting others' burdens (preferably in the form of excess gold), anything green (clothes, money, etc. . . .), staying alive, performing magic tricks

◎ **Awards & Honors**
- Sherwood Olympics: 1st place, Privy Digging
- Nottingham Fair Archery Competition: 12th place (I'm no fool!)

◎ **References**
- Friar Tuck
- Little John

Tinkerbell

Personal Statement
Ting-a-ling tink tinkety ring-a-ding. Tink-tink-tink, ring-a-tink. Triiing a-ling-tink ding-a-ring.

Highlights
- tinga-tinga-ting
- tinky-tink tink
- ling-a-ring-a-tink

Work Experience
- Tinker, ting-ding
- Tinker ding-a-ling, ringety-ting

Interests
tinkety-trink, ting-a-bink, ting-a-ring-a-tink-ting-tink, rinkety-ring, bink-a-ling

References
- Peter Pan

The Frog Prince

Personal Statement
I would jump at the chance to become your bedtime storyteller. My expertly told tales will leave your friends green with envy.

Highlights
- tells a hopping good story
- will keep your bedroom bug-free
- can fetch books (and any other trinkets) from hard-to-reach shelves

Interests
reading, eating flies with friends, swimming

Awards & Honors
- 1st Annual Summer Swamp Games: Gold Medal in Leap Frog
- Green County Fair Fly-Eating Contest: Grand Champion

References
- None at this time (a moment of silence for all of my friends lost in the name of frog-legs dinner specials)

Bedtime stories are routine in Janet Sumner Johnson's home, though she may have been fired as said storyteller once or twice. (Okay, three times, but who's counting?) Happily, she has weaseled her way back into her kids' good graces, and they occasionally allow her to fill that position (at least when Daddy isn't home). This is Johnson's debut picture book. She lives in Logan, Utah, with her husband and three kids.

Courtney Dawson is an illustrator and picture book artist living in the sunny little town of Ventura, California. She has a deep love of reading, her mom's chilaquiles, and most kinds of ice cream. Her work is inspired by the world around us and all the good that's in it. When she's not working, she can be found riding her bike, painting to Sam Cooke's music, or enjoying a rainy day with her partner, her baby, and her cute cat, Tuesday.